Flutterby

Hornetto

Buttercup

Diggly

Grubby

Violet

Daisy

Slugsy

Bumble

Mo

Fifi
and the **Flowertots**

This Fifi and
the Flowertots
Annual 2010
belongs to

Holly

....

....

First published in UK by HarperCollins Children's Books in 2009
1 3 5 7 9 10 8 6 4 2
ISBN-13: 978-0-00-732550-4

A CIP catalogue record for this title is available from the British Library.

Created by Keith Chapman
Based on the television series Fifi and the Flowertots, © Chapman Entertainment Limited 2009

Visit Fifi at www.Fifiandtheflowertots.com

Printed and bound by Leo Paper Products Ltd, China

Fifi and the Flowertots
Annual 2010

HarperCollins *Children's Books*

Hello there, I'm Fifi Forget-Me-Not!

Welcome to Flowertot Garden! I am so happy you have come to visit. You can meet all my friends and join us for lots of stories and activities.

Would you like to hear about the talent show we had? Then you can make some instruments and play along with us! Or how about the time we had a Midsummer Ball in the garden? Everyone looked so lovely that day!

We have also got lots of ideas and games to keep you entertained, whatever the weather in your garden.

Don't forget to come back soon!

 x

Contents

08 ✿ Unforgettable Flowertots

10 ✿ Fifi's Talent Show

22 ✿ Hornetto's Song

23 ✿ Hidden Hamper Maze

24 ✿ Making Music

26 ✿ Talent Time

28 ✿ Copy Colouring

29 ✿ B is for Bumble

30 ✿ Rainy Day Puzzles

32 ✿ Tidy Up Time

33 ✿ Pretty as a Picture

34 ✿ Sunny Day Fun

36 ✿ How Many?

37 ✿ Dressing Up

38 ✿ Belle of the Ball

50 ✿ Baking Day

52 ✿ Come and Play!

54 ✿ Flowertot Friends

56 ✿ D is for Daisy

57 ✿ Odd One Out

58 ✿ What Can You Remember?

60 ✿ Answers

Unforgettable Flowertots

Fiddly Flowerpetals! I've forgotten who everyone is! Can you help me join the dots under each of my friends to write their names?

Buttercup

Primrose

Daisy

9

Fifi's Talent Show

It was the day of the Flowertot Talent Contest! But Fifi's best friend, Bumble, was feeling a bit worried.

Bzzzzzzzzzzzz...

"Fifi, Stingo is one of the judges in the contest this year! And I just know he won't be fair," he buzzed. "Don't worry, Bumble," said Fifi kindly, "just try your best." Fifi hadn't decided what to do for the contest, so Bumble flew off to put her name down as a 'surprise' act.

Violet and Primrose were busy getting everything ready.

"Bouncing Blueberries!" cried Bumble when he saw the star prize – a delicious hamper from Aunt Tulip!

Stingo was peering through his telescope to see what was going on, while Slugsy was snoring peacefully in the hammock. Then Stingo had one of his naughtiest ideas...

"SLUGSYYYYYYY!"

he called, in his loudest voice. "Ouch!" cried Slugsy as he woke with a start and tumbled out of the hammock, landing with a big

BUMP!

"Yes, boss?" mumbled Slugsy. "Listen, you slimy slug, I want you to write a poem and win the hamper in this daft talent contest," instructed Stingo. "But I'm not any good at writing 'pomes'," replied Slugsy. "It's a po-em. Anyway, it doesn't matter, I'm one of the judges. I'll make sure you win!" said Stingo craftily.

Fifi was still thinking about what she could do for the contest when there was a knock at the door. It was Primrose and Violet. "Can you come to our house..." began Primrose. ".... and help us get ready for the talent contest?" finished Violet.

Back at Stingo's house, Slugsy was trying his best to write his poem.

He read the start of it to Stingo... "Baa baa black ssslug, have you any ssslime?" "I think you need to start again!" sighed Stingo.

Over at Flowertot Cottage,
Fifi watched Primrose
practise her modelling.
"Brilliant, Primrose."
said Fifi.
"But how can I make it
better?"
wondered Primrose.
"Well, maybe you could wear
a...a oh Fiddly Flowerpetals!
What's it called?
You wear it round
your neck..."

"A scarf?" guessed Violet.
"No. They're pretty and sparkly..."
said Fifi.
"Oh! A necklace?" asked Violet
and Primrose.
"A necklace! Yes," nodded Fifi at last.
"Fifi Forget-Me-Not Forgot!"
they giggled!
Then it was Violet's turn to
practise her dancing

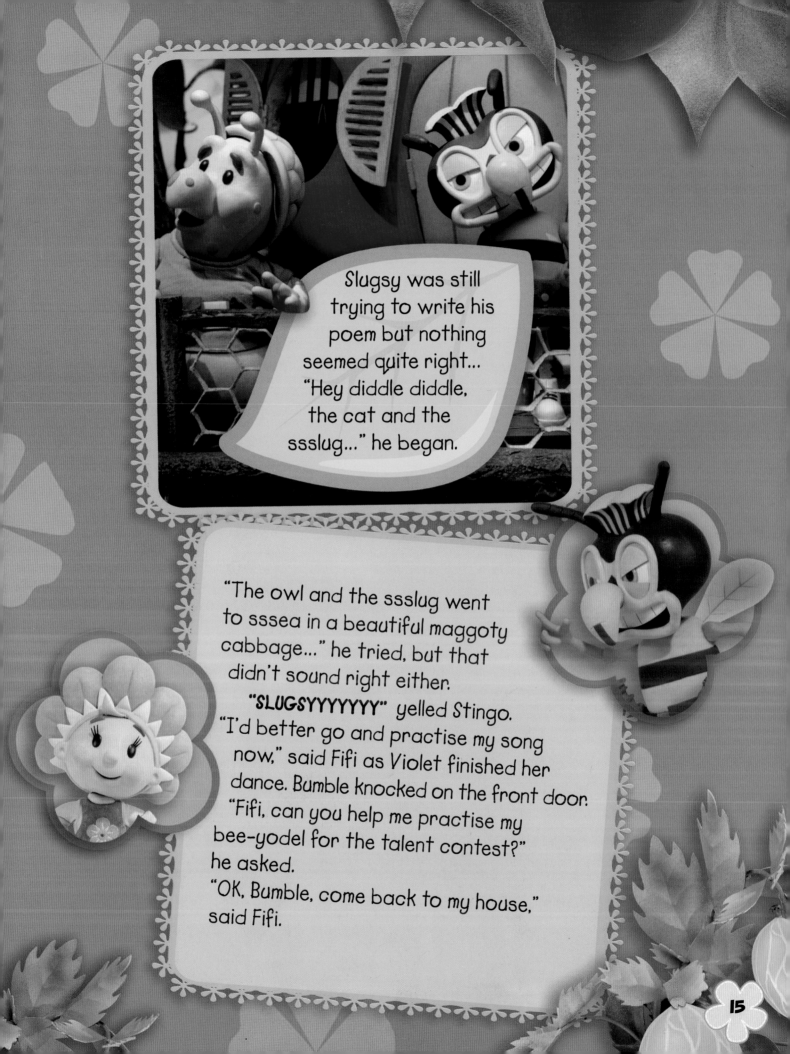

Slugsy was still trying to write his poem but nothing seemed quite right... "Hey diddle diddle, the cat and the ssslug..." he began.

"The owl and the ssslug went to sssea in a beautiful maggoty cabbage..." he tried, but that didn't sound right either.

"SLUGSYYYYYYY" yelled Stingo. "I'd better go and practise my song now," said Fifi as Violet finished her dance. Bumble knocked on the front door. "Fifi, can you help me practise my bee-yodel for the talent contest?" he asked.

"OK, Bumble, come back to my house," said Fifi.

Slugsy was still trying to come up with a poem idea when he saw Primrose and Violet on their way to the contest. **"Oooh Primrose,"** breathed Slugsy dreamily as he watched his favourite Flowertot go by.

"That's it Slugsy! Why don't you write a poem for Primrose?" beamed Stingo. "Oh yesss!" cried Slugsy, "that will be easssy!"

Fifi was helping Bumble with his yodelling. "Yodel-eee buzzy beee...," buzzed Bumble. "Hmm. Maybe try it a bit louder, Bumble," suggested Fifi. It was almost time for the contest to begin! "Oh, dear. I haven't had time to practise my song," cried Fifi.

"Diddly Dandelions, what am I going to do?" wondered Fifi as she arrived at the contest.
Slugsy clutched his poem nervously.
"That hamper's as good as mine," whispered Stingo.
"Huh?" said Slugsy.
"I mean 'ours'. Share it out and all that," added Stingo quickly.

Primrose went first with her modelling act. Next came Violet with her dancing and Bumble and his yodelling show. At last it was time for Slugsy's poem.
"It's called 'Poem for Primrose'," he said.
"How embarrassing!" blushed Primrose as Slugsy began to read aloud.

"You are a lovely Flowertot, In fact I like you...a lot! I'm just a ssslug and full of sssslime, But Primrose, you alwaysss look divine."
"Top Toffee Apples!" clapped Stingo wildly.
"Your turn, Fifi," said Bumble.
"Um...the thing is...I was so busy helping you all that...I haven't practised my song. I'm afraid I'll look silly," said Fifi quietly.
"No you won't, Fifi! You helped us and now we're going to help **YOU!**" smiled Bumble.

Bumble, Primrose and Violet joined as Fifi took to the stage.

"Get ready to shake your petals..." she said happily. And they all sang this song together.

Do you know...
this is what I say...
when I forget...

Fiddly Flowerpetals

If the sky's not blue or
it starts to rain I say

**FIDDLY FLOWERPETALS
OOO - AHH**

If I'm thinking of a word but
it somehow slips away

**FIDDLY FLOWERPETALS
OOO - AHH**

It's what I say, when I forget
Ah, ha-ha
Fiddly Flowerpetals

**FIDDLY FLOWERPETALS
FIDDLY FLOWERPETALS
FIDDLY FLOWERPETALS
FIDDLY FLOWERPETALS**
It's what I say, when I forget
It's what I do, it's what I say
Ah ha ha

**FIDDLY FLOWERPETALS
OOO - AHH**

At the end, everyone clapped with excitement. Soon, it was time for the winner to be announced.

"No contest. The slug's a genius!" said Stingo firmly. "Slugsy wins the hamper!"

"Time to share
the hamper," Stingo
whispered to Slugsy.
"You grab it and meet me back
at Apple Tree House. Stingo
flew off feeling very pleased.
But Slugsy looked at the Flowertots.
"Hmmm. I've got a better idea,"
he thought.

Slugsy decided to share his prize
with everyone!
"Thank you, Slugsy!" said Primrose fondly.
Stingo flew back and was NOT happy.
"But you sssaid ssshare it out, Bosss!"
replied Slugsy.
"Rotten Raspberries!" cried Stingo.
"I meant with **ME!!!**"
Fifi giggled. "Slugsy's learnt a
new talent today – sharing with
his friends!"

21

Hornetto's Song

Oh no! Hornetto missed the talent show! Colour this picture of him practising for the next one.

22

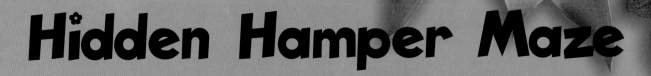

Hidden Hamper Maze

The star prize for the talent show was a delicious hamper from Aunt Tulip.
Help Slugsy through the maze to find his prize.

Making Music

Why not put on your own talent show with your friends?
Here are some ideas for musical instruments to make and play!

Fifi's Musical Maracas

You will need:
* Strips of newspaper * Yoghurt pots * Sticky tape
Dry beans or rice * Putty * Papier-mâché paste
* Paints * Scissors

To make the paste, mix $\frac{1}{2}$ a cup of plain flour and 2 cups of cold water. Ask a grown-up to add 2 cups of boiling water and to bring to the boil again as they keep stirring. Ask the grown-up to take it off the heat and stir in 3 tablespoons of sugar. When it is cool, it's ready to use!

1. Roll a strip of newspaper tightly around a pencil. Slip the pencil out and tape the ends of the newspaper. You made a handle!

2. Put the beans or rice into the container. Cut an X in the lid (a grown-up's job). Put a ball of putty on the end of the handle and wedge into the hole in the lid, pushing against the bottom of the container. Tape the handle in place.

3. Dip a strip of newspaper into the paste and wrap around the maraca. Repeat, covering the container and handle. When your maraca dries, it's ready to shake! Paint it with your brightest colours!

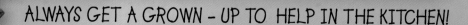

ALWAYS GET A GROWN - UP TO HELP IN THE KITCHEN!

Drums are so much fun. Remember not to bang them too hard though or Stingo might come and take them away!

Make Your Own Drums

You will need:
* Some large cans * Several layers of coloured paper
* Some glue * Some rubber bands * Colouring paints or crayons
* Pencils with rubbers on the end as drum sticks
* Wax paper or vinyl!

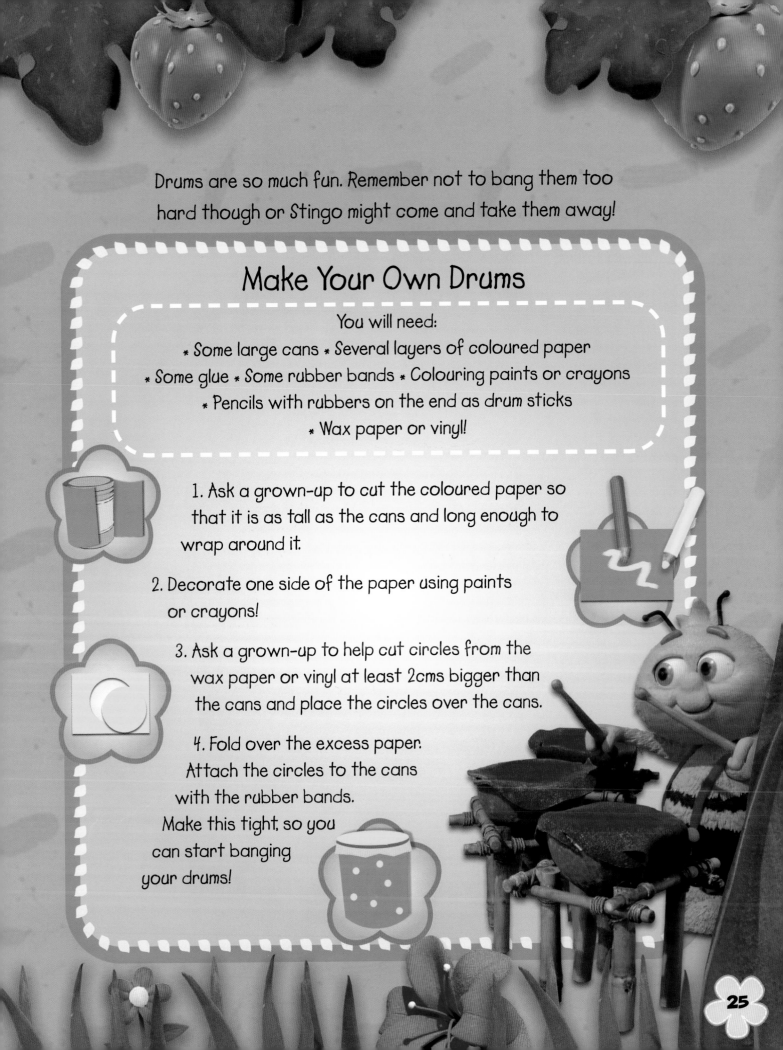

1. Ask a grown-up to cut the coloured paper so that it is as tall as the cans and long enough to wrap around it.

2. Decorate one side of the paper using paints or crayons!

3. Ask a grown-up to help cut circles from the wax paper or vinyl at least 2cms bigger than the cans and place the circles over the cans.

4. Fold over the excess paper. Attach the circles to the cans with the rubber bands. Make this tight, so you can start banging your drums!

Talent Time

Come and play this talent show game with us! Take turns rolling the die and moving the number of places shown around the board. If you land on a place with writing on, follow the instructions. The first player to reach the end of the board is the winner of the talent show!

You will need:
* Friends to play with
* A counter each
* A die

1 Start

2

3

4

5 Do a dance like Violet

6

7

8

9 Pose like Primrose the model

18 Yodel like Bumble

19

20

10

21

11

17

22 Say a rhyme like Slugsy

12

16

13

23

15

24

14 Sing a song like Fifi

25 Finish

Copy Colouring

Look at Fifi's pretty dress. Colour the big picture to match the little one.

How many flowers can you count in the picture?

28

B is for Bumble

Bumble's name begins with the letter B. How many other things can you think of that begin with B? Draw them here.

Rainy Day Puzzles
Diggly's Wordsearch

Help Diggly collect all the fruits in the list so he can add the waste to his compost heap.

```
S W R Y U I O P S G H
K L M N B V L E M O N
C D S A G H J U Y O E
P O I U Y T R E W S Q
A S D F G S H J K E M
N B V G T T Q A Z B W
S A E D O R A N G E C
R P V T G A B Y H R N
U P M I K W O L P R E
B L A C K B E R R Y I
L E P L O E K N I J U
H R B V Y R C R E R Y
T H N J U R E D B Y T
O I B Y T Y L X T R D
```

Apple
Blackberry
Gooseberry
Lemon
Orange
Strawberry

30

Spot the Difference

Poppy is busy delivering food from her market stall.
Can you spot five differences between these two pictures of her?

Tidy Up Time

Webby is cleaning her web, ready for a visit from Aunt Tulip. Help her by circling four things that don't belong there.

32

Pretty as a Picture

Violet has painted some lovely flowers. Use the canvas below to draw or paint your own flowers.

Sunny Day Fun

Hooray! The sun is shining in Flowertot Garden. Here are some of our favourite games to play outside on a nice day. Why don't you try them too?

Stingo Says

This is a great game to play with lots of friends. Choose one person to call out instructions, using the words "Stingo says..." For example, they might say "Stingo says hop up and down!" or "Stingo says spin in a circle."

Everyone has to do whatever Stingo says. But, if the caller does not say "Stingo says" before the instruction, then everyone has to stand still as a statue! Anyone who follows the wrong instructions is out of the game!

Flower Tag

This is a chasing game for three or more players. One person is the chaser and should stand a short distance away from the other players, all at one end of the garden. Each person thinks of a different flower and whispers it to everyone else except the chaser. The chaser then has to call out the names of flowers. If someone's flower is called, they must run to the other end of the garden and back, with the chaser chasing them. If the runner is tagged, they become the chaser. If not, the runner sits out and the chaser keeps calling out flowers until they catch someone or run out of players.

Slugsy in the Middle

You will need a ball and three players for this game. Two players throw the ball to each other, with the third player in the middle trying to catch it. If the middle player catches the ball, they swap places with the person who threw it and they become the Slugsy in the middle!

Fifi's Scavenger Hunt

There are lots of interesting things to be found in any garden. Why not have a scavenger hunt and see if you can find all the things on my list? You could have two teams and see who manages to collect everything first. When you have completed my list, create your own or ask a grown-up to make one for you.

Fifi's List
A leaf
A round stone
A twig
A feather
A flower petal

How Many?

Help Buttercup count up all the objects in each row.

Write the numbers in the flowers.

Dressing Up

Fifi has the perfect outfit for every occasion, but sometimes she forgets which one she should wear! Help her decide by matching her clothes to the best time to wear them.

1

2

A. A rainy day
B. Time for bed
C. A party
D. A cold day

3

4

Belle of the Ball

It was a bright summer's day in Flowertot Garden. Fifi was visiting Poppy's Market Stall, where she met Violet and Aunt Tulip.

"Hello Aunt Tulip," Fifi waved.
"What are you doing at the market?

"Sweet Potatoes Child!

I'm getting ready for tonight's Midsummer Flowertot Ball," she replied.

"Buttercups and Daisies!

I forgot!" Fifi said, as the others laughed.
"What are you going to wear?"
Violet asked.
"Oh I don't know," Fifi laughed, "I'm far too busy to worry about dressing up. It's what you feel like, not what you look like that is important."

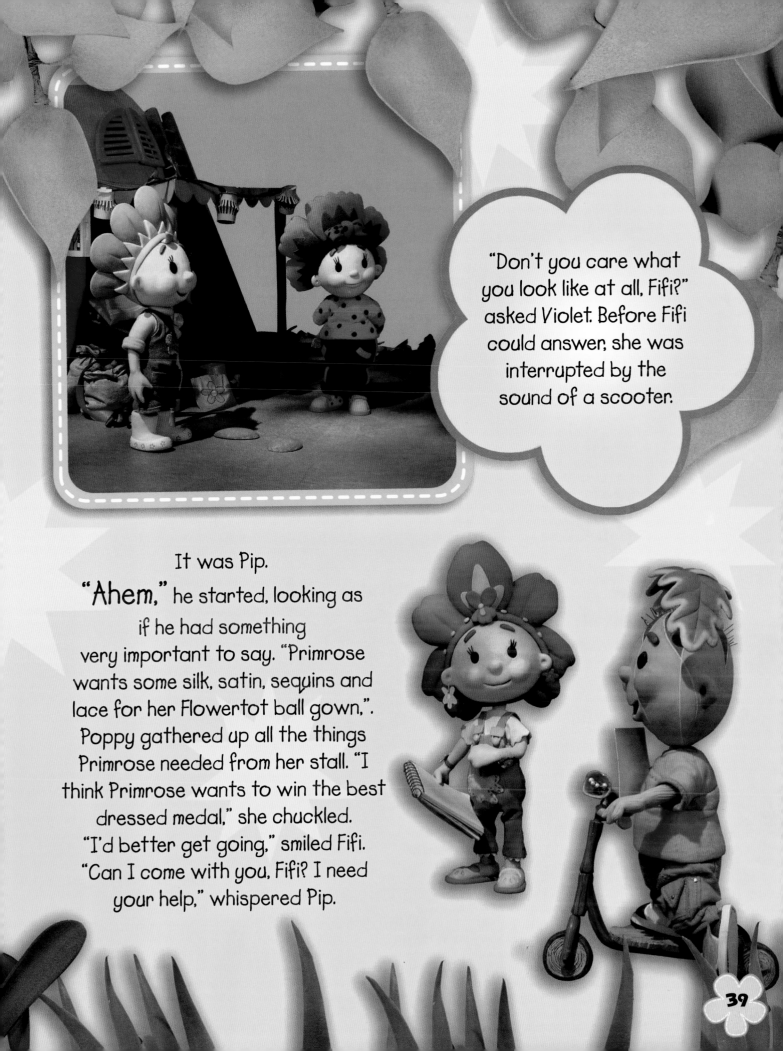

"Don't you care what you look like at all, Fifi?" asked Violet. Before Fifi could answer, she was interrupted by the sound of a scooter.

It was Pip.

"Ahem," he started, looking as if he had something very important to say. "Primrose wants some silk, satin, sequins and lace for her Flowertot ball gown,". Poppy gathered up all the things Primrose needed from her stall. "I think Primrose wants to win the best dressed medal," she chuckled. "I'd better get going," smiled Fifi. "Can I come with you, Fifi? I need your help," whispered Pip.

"I want to look good for the ball," began Pip,
"but I don't know what to wear."
Fifi looked thoughtful for a moment. "What
about wearing a cloak and you can go as Pip
Prince Charming," she suggested.
"I like that!" beamed Pip, "I'll go and see
what I can find!"
With that, he hurried off.

Back in her garden, Fifi found Bumble holding up a
stripy tie and a bow tie.

"Bouncing Buttercups, Fifi!"

he buzzed excitedly. "I don't know what
to wear tonight!"
"Not you too, Bumble," Fifi sighed.
"But which tie should I wear?"
Bumble asked.
"They're both nice. I know, go and ask Primrose.
She always knows what's good to wear."
"Good idea!" said Bumble and buzzed
off happily.

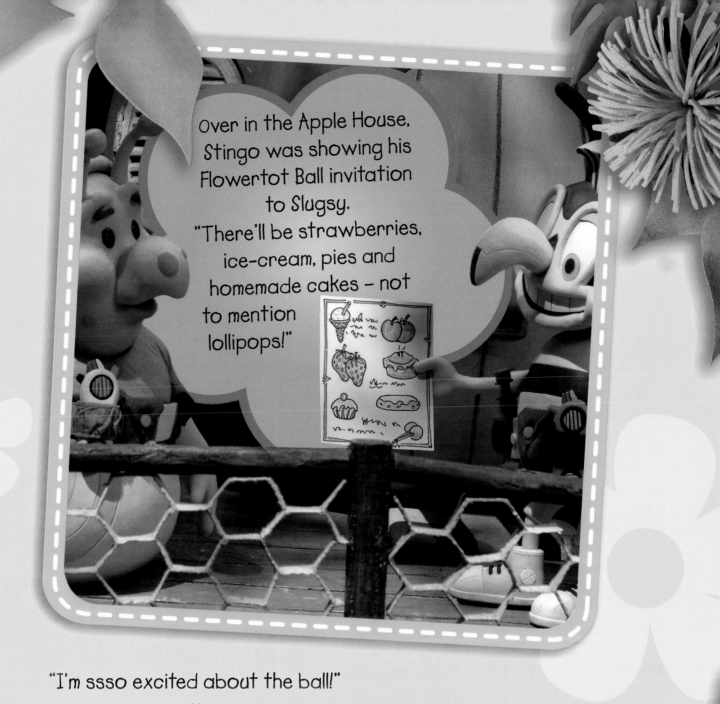

Over in the Apple House, Stingo was showing his Flowertot Ball invitation to Slugsy. "There'll be strawberries, ice-cream, pies and homemade cakes – not to mention lollipops!"

"I'm ssso excited about the ball!" said Slugsy.
"But **you** can't go to a ball like **that!**" Stingo said, shaking his head.
Slugsy looked very disappointed. "How elssse can I go, SSStingo?" he asked.
"Oh slug of very little brain! You have to dress up!" said Stingo. He looked hard at Slugsy. "And we're going to need a lot of material to cover you!"

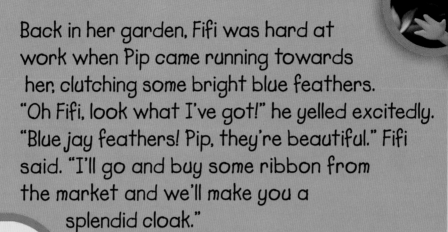

Back in her garden, Fifi was hard at work when Pip came running towards her, clutching some bright blue feathers. "Oh Fifi, look what I've got!" he yelled excitedly. "Blue jay feathers! Pip, they're beautiful." Fifi said. "I'll go and buy some ribbon from the market and we'll make you a splendid cloak."

But Fifi wasn't the only one going to market. Just as she arrived, Stingo buzzed towards the stall.

BUZZZZZZZZZZZZZZZ!

"I'm looking for some material Poppy. In fact – I'm looking for a lot of material," he said. "It's a surprise for Slugsy," he whispered to Fifi.

"I hope it's a nice surprise, Stingo," Fifi said sternly.

"On my wasp's honour, it's a very nice surprise!" said Stingo as he buzzed off.

Soon Slugsy was draped in the bright, red material.

"Do I look pretty, SSStingo?" Slugsy posed for his friend.

"No!" said Stingo, "but at least it covers you."

"Will you dance with me?" Slugsy asked, dipping in a huge curtsey. "We've got to practissse or we won't be able to dance at the ball."

"I'm not dancing with a slug!" cried Stingo.

Slugsy gave Stingo his sweetest look.

"Oh, alright then," Stingo agreed.

"Laaah, laaah, laaah," sang Slugsy, as he dragged Stingo around the terrace in a bumpy waltz.

"Oh, Rotten Raspberries!" grumbled Stingo.

It was almost time for the ball and Pip
and Fifi were making his outfit.
        In no time at all, Pip had a handsome
        blue jay feather cloak, tied to his
        shoulders by a beautiful
        purple ribbon.
            "Thank you Fifi, see you
            at the Flowertot ball!"
Pip said.
            "Bye bye, handsome
            Pip Prince Charming,"
            waved Fifi.

Pip had barely left the garden
    when Bumble buzzed in,
        flourishing a flashy bow
        tie. "I've decided to
        wear this one, Fifi!"
        he said.
            "And you should see
            Primrose's dress, it's

gorrrrrr-geous."

"Fussing over clothes is very silly," Fifi said to herself as Bumble buzzed off, "but if everyone else is making an effort to look their best..."
Fifi looked down at her dungarees. "What should I wear?"
She plopped down on the ground and looked around her garden until her eyes landed on the lovely flowers all around her.

"Buttercups and Daisies!"

she laughed. "I've had a fantastic Flowertot idea!"

Later that evening, Fifi arrived at the
Flowertot Midsummer Ball. Everyone turned
and stared at her beautiful ball gown made
entirely from flower petals!
"Will you dance with me, Princess Fifi?"
asked Pip with a deep bow.

"With pleasure, Pip Prince Charming!"
giggled Fifi.
All the Flowertots began to dance
around Fifi and Pip, except for
Stingo and Slugsy. They were far
too busy feasting on the cakes,
jellies, sandwiches and lollipops!

46

It didn't take long before Stingo and Slugsy began to feel a little sick.

"My tummy hurts!" groaned Slugsy as they tried to sneak off while everyone was dancing.

"And where are you two going?" asked Fifi.

"Home, we feel sick," moaned Stingo. They both looked terrible!

"**Fiddly Flowerpetals!** If you hadn't been so greedy you could have stayed and danced all night," Fifi said, watching them stagger off.

"We'll remember that next time," Stingo muttered.

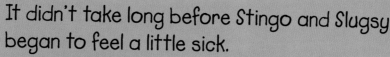

"You all look so beautiful." Aunt Tulip had started her speech. It was time to announce the winner of the best dressed Flowertot medal "But somebody's got to win, so the best dressed medal goes to Pip for his fabulous blue cloak!" Aunt Tulip smiled and handed the medal to Pip as everyone clapped and cheered.

47

"Thank you!" Pip said, "but if it weren't for Fifi, I wouldn't have had anything to wear to the ball so I'm going to give my medal to Fifi Forget-Me-Not!"

Pip carefully placed the medal around Fifi's neck. "Because not only is she kind, she's also the Flowertot Belle of the Ball!"
"Thank you!" she blushed as everyone clapped and cheered for Fifi Forget-Me-Not, Flowertot Belle of the Ball.

Baking Day

Buttercups and Daisies! I love to bake and jam tarts are my favourite treat to make. Ask a grown-up to help you make some of your own!

You will need:

* A jar of jam (I like strawberry best!)
* 150g/5.3oz plain flour
* 75g/2.6oz butter or margarine, cut into small cubes
* 1tbsp sugar
* A little water
* Mixing bowl
* Sieve
* Tablespoon
* Teaspoon
* Rolling pin
* Round pastry cutter
* Jam tart baking tray, greased with a little butter
* Clean hands!

1. Ask a grown-up to preheat the oven to 190°C, 380°F or gas mark 5.

2. Sift the flour and sugar into the mixing bowl and add the cubes of butter or margarine.

3. Rub everything together until the mixture looks like breadcrumbs.

4. Mix in some cold water one tablespoonful at a time, until the mixture forms a dough. If it gets too sticky, add a little more flour.

5. Sprinkle some flour on a clean surface and roll out the pastry.

6. With the help of a grown-up, cut out as many circles as you can and put them in the greased baking tray.

7. Add one teaspoon of jam to each pastry case.

8. Ask a grown-up to put them in the oven and cook for five minutes or until the pastry is golden brown.

9. When they are ready, ask the grown-up to remove the jam tarts from the oven for you and leave them to cool. Jam gets very hot, so wait until the tarts are completely cold before you enjoy them!

Come and Play!

1. How many Flowertots are playing in the garden?
10

2. What colour
are the flowers?
orange

3. What fruit is
growing on
the bush?
gooseberrys

Point to your
favourite
Flowertot.
FiFi

Flowertot Friends

Use your crayons or felt-tip pens to colour the pictures of Fifi's Flowertot friends.

54

55

D is for Daisy

Daisy's name begins with the letter D. How many other things can you think of that begin with D? Draw them in here.

Odd One Out

Help Hornetto circle the odd one out in each group of objects.

What Can You Remember?

Fiddly Flowerpetals! How much can you remember from this annual? Answer the questions below to find out.

1. Circle the winner of the talent show.

2. Who appears on the cover with Fifi?

b.

c.

d.

3. What did you paint with Violet?

4. What kind of weather should I wear this outfit in?

a. Sunny
b. Rainy
c. Snowy

5. How many apples did you count with Buttercup?

a. One
b. Two
c. Three

6. Who won the best dressed medal but gave their prize to Fifi?

PiP

Answers

PAGE 23

Hidden

Hamper Maze

PAGE 30

Diggly's

Wordsearch

PAGE 31

Spot the

Difference

PAGE 32

Tidy Up

Time

PAGE 36

How Many?

1. 3 apples

2. 5 jars

3. 4 presents

4. 6 lollies

PAGE 37

Dressing Up

A. 1

B. 3

C. 2

D. 4

PAGE 52

Come and Play!

1. 10

2. Orange

3. Gooseberries

PAGE 57

Odd One Out

1. Paintbrush

2. Radish

3. Spoon

4. Pink coloured flower

PAGE 58

What Can You Remember?

1. Slugsy won the talent show.

2. Buttercup and Daisy.

3. Flowers.

4. My raincoat is for rainy days.

5. Buttercup counted three apples.

6. Pip.

Subscribe Today and Save!

Subscribe today and save 10%, just £11.60 for 6 issues!

For more details and to subscribe, call 0844 856 0646 (overseas +44 (0)1795 414 904)
quoting FIANNUAL or go online and enter this code at www.titantots.com

CHECK OUT
our other great
Pre-school magazines...

Fifi

Stingo

Webby

Primrose

Aunt Tulip

Poppy

Pip